Lizzy
Lizard

BOOKS BY HOUSE OF NEHESI PUBLISHERS

The Frock & Other Poems
Laurel "Yaya" Richards

Because of Prayer
Felecita T. Williams

Hakuna Matata & Other Travel Stories
Gerard van Veen

Claude's Adventure
Wendy-Ann Diaz

37 Poems
Lasana M. Sekou

Songs & Images of St. Martin
Charles Borromeo Hodge

Tales From the Great Salt Pond
Esther Gumbs

National Symbols of St. Martin –
A Primer
Edited by Lasana M. Sekou

Pass it on!
A Treasury of Virgin Islands Tales
Jennie N. Wheatley

Golden Voices of S'maatin
Ruby Bute

Love Songs Make Cry
Lasana M. Sekou

PIONEER SERIES

Mr. Bibi
Pioneer in House Drawing & Design

Lambee
& The Road That Couldn't Be Built

Chester York
Making of a Pan Man

Father Alfie
Faith is ... Assent to Revelation

Gassy
Champion Cyclist

Lizzy Lizard

Robin Boasman

HOUSE OF NEHESI PUBLISHERS   ST MARTIN · CARIBBEAN

HOUSE OF NEHESI PUBLISHERS
P.O. Box 460
Philipsburg, St. Martin
Caribbean

www.houseofnehesipublish.com

© 2013 by Robin Boasman
ISBN: 9780988825215
LC Control Number: 2013900199

Acknowledgment: This book has been made possible in part through a grant from the Ministry of Education, Culture, Sports and Youth Affairs. Special thanks from the author "To my mother 'Teacher Ans' Rijnboutt and father Rafael Boasman; Sheira Richardson; and Dr. Rhoda Arrindell, whose class lectures and assignments planted and developed the idea for this book in 2009."

Photo art illustrations: Sea grape tree, p. vi; University of St. Martin campus, p. 3; Saltpickers monument, WJA Nisbeth Road, p. 5; The zoo, Arch Road, pp. 12-13; A flamboyant overlooking the city of Philipsburg, traditionally called Great Bay — showing part of The Great Salt Pond, Fresh Pond, Great Bay Harbor, A.T. Illidge Road, Zagersgut Road, Bush Road, and Fort Hill, pp. 18-19; Long Wall Road with mangroves on the bank of the Fresh Pond, p. 23; Little Bay peninsula, with ruins of Fort Amsterdam in the foreground, pp. 28-29; University of St. Martin campus, p. 31; The Brown Pelican, the "National Bird," wings outstretched in St. Martin skies, p. 33.

Cover and book design: BEO Studios, Inc.
Photography: Robert J. Cijntje, Angelo Rombley, Saltwater Collection, Robin Boasman.

To Naheem Brown, my son

There's a little lizard living in St. Martin. This little lizard's name is Lizzy. Lizzy Lizard.
She lives in a sea grape tree on the grounds of the University of St. Martin in Philipsburg.

1

During the day as workers were busy building and adding new classrooms, it was too noisy, so she had to leave her tree house. Because Lizzy had to leave home every day to get away from the noise, she sometimes got bored. Running around the university grounds, jumping on the workers' tools, searching the students' bags, climbing into the offices of the teachers, and biting the fruits on the trees before they were all ripe usually got her into trouble.

One day Lizzy decided to take a long walk. She hoped to make some new friends. Lizzy left her home and headed for Frontstreet. She skipped past the salt pickers' statues, patting each one as she went by. When she reached in front of the Court House, she climbed to the roof. Lizzy then sat on top of the gold-colored pineapple at the top of the building to watch the many people and cars moving about on the busiest city street on the island.

Soon she noticed that the beach was close by, so she decided to go look at the sea.

When she was sitting on the sand, Lizzy Lizard saw something coming toward her.

At first she could not tell what it was, but when she looked closer she saw that it was a soldier crab.

"Hi," said Lizzy. "My name is Lizzy Lizard. What's your name?"

"Hi," said the soldier crab.

"My name is Suzy Soldier Crab. What are you doing?"

"I'm just sitting here, watching the sea," said Lizzy. "I had to leave home because they are building, and it is too noisy. So I'm on an adventure to try and make new friends. Do you want to be my friend?"

"Sure," said Suzy. "It's always fun to make new friends."

Lizzy and Suzy played in the sand together for a while until Lizzy wanted to continue on her search for new friends. So she said goodbye to Suzy and walked in the direction of Sucker Garden. She decided to walk along Arch Road to go to the zoo.

Lizzy was sure that she would make a friend at the zoo. When she got there, she looked around and could not see anybody. Then suddenly she heard a deep voice behind her.

"May I help you?" Lizzy turned around quickly and saw an iguana sitting on a stone watching her.

12

She said in a friendly voice, "Hi, my name is Lizzy Lizard, and I am on an adventure to make new friends. What's your name?"

"Oooohh, my name is Iggy Iguana." He said in a deep, slow voice.

"Can I be your friend? I always wanted to have a new friend."

"Sure, Iggy," said Lizzy. She was excited that Iggy wanted to be her friend. Iggy and Lizzy hung out for a while, and Iggy gave her a tour of the zoo. She met the ostrich, the ocelot, the monkeys, and the peacock. She did not get to play with them because they were inside their houses, but she was happy to meet them.

After meeting Iggy's family and his other zoo friends, Lizzy knew it was time to continue her adventure.

She said her goodbye and went on her way along The Great Salt Pond. Lizzy was happy with the way her adventure was going. She already had two new friends.

Before Lizzy knew it, she was almost by the L.B. Scott Sports Auditorium. She crossed the street when the traffic light turned to red.

As Lizzy walked closer to the auditorium, she noticed a mongoose sitting on the Long Wall.

When Lizzy got to the mongoose she said, "Hi, my name is Lizzy Lizard. What's your name?"

She told Lizzy that her name was Missy Mongoose.

"What are you doing, Missy?" asked Lizzy.

Missy looked at her and said, "Oh nothing, really. I'm just watching the cars drive by. What are you doing, Lizzy?"

"I'm just on an adventure to make new friends."

"Sounds like fun," said Missy.

"Oh yes it is!"

23

Lizzy and Missy talked for a little while longer, but Lizzy noticed that it was getting late. She would soon have to go home, but first Lizzy wanted to make just one more friend. Lizzy told Missy that she would come back soon again to see her.

*L*izzy thought about where she would go next and finally chose to go visit Little Bay.

It did not take long before Lizzy met Pico Pelican. She first saw him flying high in the sky. When he landed and sat on the rocks, Lizzy walked over to him.

"Hi, my name is Lizzy Lizard. What's your name?"

He said, "Hi Lizzy, my name is Picolorio Picantisso Pelican, but you can call me Pico."

Pico asked, "Lizzy, how was your day?"

Lizzy thought for a little bit before she answered.

"Well Pico, my whole day was great, but I think the best part was making so many new friends. I never thought that I would make so many different friends."

Soon Lizzy had to leave, but this time her next stop would be home. She told Pico goodbye and left.

As Lizzy walked back home, she thought about her day. She was so happy with the way things had gone. The thing that made her the happiest was what she told Pico Pelican. She was glad that she made so many new kinds of friends.

The next day, Lizzy went to visit all of her new friends again.

About the Author

Robin Boasman was born in Philipsburg, St. Martin, and received her B.A. in education from the University of St. Martin. During her studies she worked as a tutor, assisting children with their homework and remedial lessons. Boasman currently teaches at the Sister Magda Primary School. According to Boasman, "it is highly important for children to read, but children will more likely read when they enjoy and can relate to what they are reading. This is how the story of Lizzy Lizard came about." Robin Boasman is a mother and *Lizzy Lizard* is her first book.